# PEDRO
## ON THE GO

by Fran Manushkin

illustrated by Tammie Lyon

CAPSTONE PRESS
a capstone imprint

Pedro is published by Picture Window Books,
a Capstone imprint
1710 Roe Crest Drive
North Mankato, Minnesota 56003
www.capstonepub.com

Text © 2021 Fran Manushkin
Illustrations © 2021 Picture Window Books

Cataloging-in-Publication Data is available on the Library of Congress website.
ISBN: 978-1-5158-7268-9 (paperback)
ISBN: 978-1-5158-7269-6 (eBook PDF)

Summary: Pedro loves going out and having fun with his friends and family. From a wild hike with his dad to an imaginary adventure on Mars with his classmates, Pedro always has an awesome time when he's on the go!

Designer: Bobbie Nuytten
Design Elements by Shutterstock

Printed and bound in the USA.
PA117

# Table of Contents

# THE
# BEST PET?

Pedro told his dog, Peppy,

"Tomorrow is the pet show.

I want you to be the best pet!

Let's practice your tricks."

Pedro told Peppy, "Sit!"

Peppy sat.

Pedro said, "Stay."

Peppy stayed.

"Fetch!" said Pedro.

Peppy fetched.

"Good dog!" Pedro smiled.

He gave Peppy a treat.

Then Pedro gave Peppy a bath.
Peppy did not like baths. He
liked mud a lot better!

The next day was the pet show.
Pedro saw Katie and her kitten,
Peaches. Peppy liked Peaches,
and Peaches liked Peppy.

Roddy told Pedro, "My parrot
Rocky will win. He is the best."

"Best! Best! BEST!" said Rocky.

Pedro waited for the judge to come and see Peppy. Pedro told Peppy, "Sit."

Peppy sat.

He sat on a bee.

TWO bees!

Peppy howled! Peppy
jumped! Peppy ran!

He ran into a mud puddle.

*SPLAT!*

Peppy began to shake. He shook mud all over Pedro.

"You two are a mess!" yelled Roddy. "No ribbons for you."

Pedro felt sad.

Pedro tried to cheer up. He
watched Pablo's hamster spinning
on his wheel.

"Great spinning!" said the judge.
Pablo won a ribbon.

Pedro saw JoJo and her bunny, Betty.

Betty won a ribbon too. She won for being soft and furry and friendly.

Then Pedro saw Katie. She said, "Peaches is shaking. She has never been to a pet show. The noise and smells are scaring her."

The judges saw Roddy's parrot.

"He's the best," bragged Roddy.

Rocky screamed, "Best! Best!
BEST!"

That made
Peaches jump.

Peaches ran away!

Katie chased Peaches, but Peaches was fast. She ran under a fence and into the woods!

Peppy ran too! He ran after
Peaches.

Pedro yelled, "Peppy, FETCH!"

Peppy jumped over the fence.

Peaches was hiding. Peppy sniffed
and sniffed. He found Peaches!

He picked her up and jumped
back over the fence.

*SPLAT!*

Peppy landed in the mud.

But he held on to Peaches.

She was safe!

Katie hugged Peaches and Peppy.

She didn't mind getting muddy.

Pedro patted Peppy over and over.

"Good dog! Good dog!"

The judge told Pedro, "You told Peppy to fetch, and he did! Peppy is the best. He wins the blue ribbon!"

"Yay!" Everyone cheered.

When Pedro and Peppy got home, they needed a bath. Guess who liked his bath better?

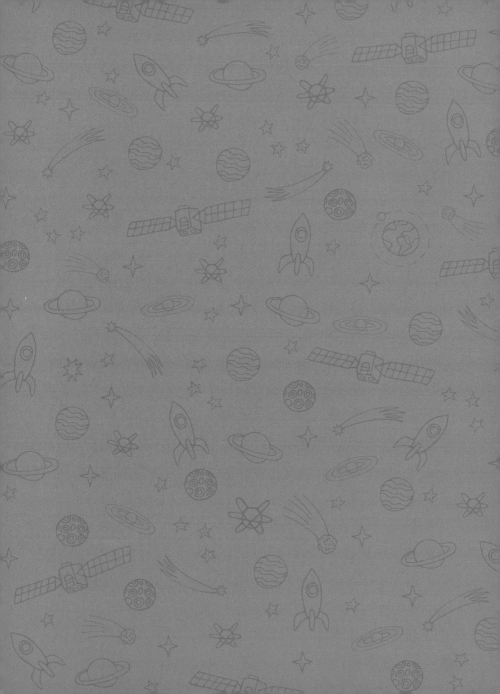

# PEDRO GOES
# TO MARS

Pedro was reading about Mars.

He told Miss Winkle, "Mars looks

cool. It would be fun to go there."

Katie raised her hand. "I want to go to Saturn. I'll ride around on its rings. I'll get nice and dizzy!"

Miss Winkle said, "You might not like it. The rings of Saturn are made of dust and ice."

"Yikes!" yelled Katie. "I'll go somewhere else."

That night, Pedro told his dad,
"I'd like to go to Mars."

"Are you sure?" asked Pedro's
dad. "It's far away."

"That's okay," said Pedro. "I have a big suitcase, and I like long trips."

"Mars is 225 million miles away," said Pedro's dad.

"No problem," said Pedro. "I'll pack lots of sandwiches."

"And bring some cows for milk,"
added Pedro's dad.

That night, Pedro dreamed
about going to Mars.

His spaceship was crowded and
noisy. The cows never slept!

The next day, Pedro read more
about Mars.

"It's very rocky," said Miss Winkle.

"Great!" Pedro smiled. "I like
climbing rocks."

The class read about Pluto too.

JoJo said, "If I lived on Pluto,
I would see five moons outside my
window."

"Wild!" said Pedro.

Katie told the class, "Saturn has 82 moons."

"No way!" said Pedro.

"It's true," said Miss Winkle. "That sky is very crowded!"

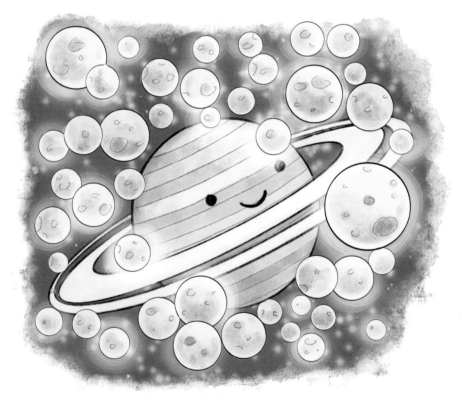

She told the class, "Each of the planets goes around the sun. How many days does it take for Earth to do it?"

Sofia, a new girl, said, "It takes 365 days."

"Right," said Pedro. "I must wait 365 days for each new birthday. That's a long time."

Later, Pedro asked his dad,
"How many days does it take
Mars to go around the sun?"

His dad looked it up. "It takes
687 days."

The next day, Pedro told Katie, "When I go to Mars, I will have to wait 687 days between birthdays."

"Wow!" said Katie. "That's a long time."

"For sure!" said Pedro.

After school, Pedro and Katie
and JoJo played soccer. The sun was
shining, and a red cardinal sang a
happy song.

Pedro said, "Earth is a very nice planet. I think I'll stay here for a while."

"Good idea," said Katie.

That night, Pedro went
to bed, smiling at the moon.
The moon smiled back!

# PEDRO KEEPS
# HIS COOL

Snow was falling—lots and lots of snow.

"Cool!" yelled Pedro. "Our winter festival will be a blast!"

Pedro met Katie at the park.
"Here comes Roddy with a
snowball," warned Katie. "Duck!"

Pedro ducked, but he still got hit.

"Come on!" said Katie. "Let's enter the snowman contest."

Katie made a snow whale.

Pedro made a snow horse.

It was a mess!

Roddy's snow dog was the best.

Pedro said, "Let's sled down the big hill. I'm a great sledder!"

"Later," said Roddy. "First, let's make snow angels."

Katie smiled. "Roddy and angels do not go together!"

"For sure!" said Pedro.

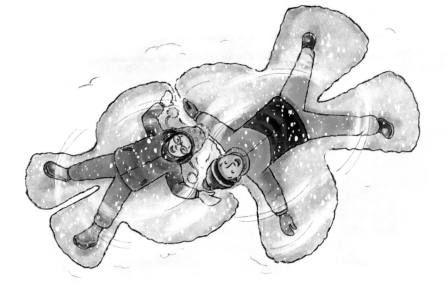

They plopped down in the snow.
Pedro said, "I know I can make a
perfect snow angel."

He didn't! But Pedro kept his cool.

"Now let's sled down the big hill," said Pedro.

"Later," said Roddy. "I want to toss the hat on the snowman."

Pedro tossed the hat. He missed the snowman.

He missed over and over. "No big deal," said Pedro.

Pedro said, "I really want to sled down the big hill. Let's go!"

"Later," said Roddy.

"You keep saying that," said Pedro.

"Let's skate first!" said Katie.

"I can skate backward,"
bragged Roddy.

"Me too!" yelled Pedro.

*Splat!* Pedro fell down.

Katie told Pedro, "Don't worry. Everyone is good at something. You are a great sledder."

"I am!" said Pedro. "Let's go."

"See you later," said Roddy. He
began walking away.

"Wait!" said Pedro. "Why don't
you want to go sledding?"

Roddy looked at the hill.

Pedro looked at Roddy.

"That hill is high," said Pedro.

"Maybe it's a little scary?"

"Maybe," said Roddy.

"Sledding can be scary at first,"
said Pedro. "But then it's cool."

He and Katie began walking up
the hill. Roddy watched them.

"Wait!" Roddy began running after Pedro. "I want to try it. Can I ride with you?"

"Sure!" said Pedro. "Hop on and hold tight!"

Roddy held tight. He held his breath too.

"Blast off!" yelled Pedro.

*Whoosh!*

They sped down the hill.

"Wow!" yelled Roddy. "Wow, wow, WOW!"

"Awesome!" yelled Pedro.

"Let's do it again!" said Roddy.

He told Pedro, "You are the best! That was so cool."

"Now let's hurry and have hot chocolate," said Pedro.

That was cool too!

# PEDRO
# GOES WILD

"It's a sunny day," said Pedro's dad. "How about a hike?"

"Cool!" said Pedro. "I love the woods. We can be wild."

"Don't worry about getting lost,"
said Pedro's dad. "I'm a great hiker."
"Good!" said Pedro.
They began to walk.

"These leaves are pretty," said Pedro's dad. "Let's pick some for Mom."

"Stop!" yelled Pedro. "That's poison ivy."

"Wow!" said Pedro's dad. "That was scary."

"Not as scary as bears," said Pedro. "I hope we don't see any."

"Oh boy!" said his dad. "If I saw a bear, I would try flying away like that crow."

"That's not a crow," said Pedro. "It's a hawk."

"He's fierce!"
said Pedro's dad.

"For sure," said
Pedro. "Hawks like
to eat rats."

"Yuck!" said Pedro's dad.
"I wouldn't!"

"Let's run now," said Pedro.

His dad ran fast. Suddenly he yelled, "STOP! I see a bear!"

The bear was . . . a sweet, fuzzy dog!

Pedro's dad laughed and laughed. So did Pedro.

"Now, let's eat," said
Pedro's dad.

"Your peanut butter sandwich
is terrific," said Pedro. "Now, I
need a drink."

"Uh-oh!" said his dad. "I forgot to
fill the canteen."

Pedro asked, "Dad, did you ever
hike before?"

His dad smiled. "A long time ago."

"Let's give these ants a sandwich," said Pedro.

The ants ate all of it. They didn't need a drink.

Pedro and his dad began walking again.

"Yikes!" yelled Pedro's dad. "Something big just jumped on my leg."

He ran in a panic and fell in a puddle!

"It's only a frog," said Pedro.

"It can't hurt you."

"Oh my!" His dad laughed. "I am a terrible hiker."

Pedro looked up at the sky.

"Uh-oh," he said. "A storm is
coming! Let's hurry home."

"We came on this path,"
said Pedro's dad.

They began walking. It was
the wrong path! Lightning started!
And thunder!

"Don't worry!" said Pedro.

"I think I know the right way.

But I can't run as fast as you.

Can you carry me?"

"Sure I can," said Pedro's dad.

He began running.

Uphill! Then downhill!

And uphill again!

Pedro's dad was strong and fast.

He ran like the wind.

"Go, Daddy!" yelled Pedro.

At home, Pedro's dad said, "I'm sorry I didn't know much about hiking."

Pedro shook his head. "Dad, you know the most important thing."

"What's that?" asked Pedro's dad.

"You know how to have fun!" said Pedro.

"I do!" His dad beamed.

They hugged on it.

# JOKE AROUND

🍃 What is a dog's favorite dessert?
pupcakes

🍃 Knock, knock.
**Who's there?**
Ken
**Ken who?**
Ken you walk the dog for me?

🍃 What do you call a pile of kittens?
a meowntain

🍃 Why are cats great singers?
They are very mewsical.

# WITH PEDRO!

Why did the cow go to outer space? It wanted to go to the moooooooon!

How do you know when the moon has enough to eat? It's full.

What did Mars say to Saturn? Give me a ring sometime.

How do you throw a birthday party in space? You have to PLAN-et.

# JOKE AROUND

❄ **What do you call a snowman temper tantrum?**
a meltdown

❄ **Where do snowmen go to dance?**
the snowball

❄ **What do snowmen have for breakfast?**
Frosted Snowflakes

❄ **What often falls in the winter but never gets hurt?**
snow

🍁 Which side of a tree has the most leaves?
the outside

🍁 Why did Humpty Dumpty have a great fall?
Because he enjoyed all the colorful leaves while hiking.

🍁 What did the hikers call the bear with no teeth?
a gummy bear

🍁 Have you heard the joke about the skunk and the hiking trip?
Never mind—it really stinks.

## About the Author

Fran Manushkin is the author of Katie Woo, the highly acclaimed fan-favorite early reader series, as well as the popular Pedro series. Her other books include *Happy in Our Skin, Baby, Come Out!* and the best-selling board books *Big Girl Panties* and *Big Boy Underpants*. There is a real Katie Woo: Fran's great-niece, but she doesn't get into as much trouble as the Katie in the books. Fran lives in New York City, three blocks from Central Park, where she can often be found bird-watching and daydreaming. She writes at her dining room table, without the help of her naughty cats, Goldy and Chaim.

## About the Illustrator

Tammie Lyon began her love for drawing at a young age while sitting at the kitchen table with her dad. She continued her love of art and eventually attended the Columbus College of Art and Design, where she earned a bachelor's degree in fine art. After a brief career as a professional ballet dancer, she decided to devote herself full time to illustration. Today she lives with her husband, Lee, in Cincinnati, Ohio. Her dogs, Gus and Dudley, keep her company as she works in her studio.